TERRIFIC

STORY AND PICTURES BY JON AGEE

Michael di Capua Books · Hyperion

Copyright © 2005 by Jon Agee   Library of Congress control number: 2004117133

First edition, 2005   Third printing, 2006

Much to his surprise, Eugene was the lucky winner of an all-expenses-paid cruise to Bermuda. "Terrific," he said. "I'll probably get a really nasty sunburn."

But on the way there, the ship ran into a terrible storm. Everyone was rescued, except for Eugene. "Terrific," he said. "I'll probably get devoured by sharks."

Instead, Eugene washed up on a tiny island. "Terrific," he said. "Now I'll get eaten by cannibals." But when he looked around, nobody else was there.

Except for a parrot.
"Terrific," said Eugene. "What good is a parrot?"
"You'd be surprised," said the parrot.

Eugene *was* surprised.
"Uh, are you stranded on this island too?"
"Afraid so," said the parrot. "My wing is busted."

"I guess we're both out of luck," said Eugene.
"Anything around here to eat?"
"Plenty of pomegranates," said the parrot.
"Terrific," said Eugene. "I hate pomegranates!
 Anything to drink?"
"Pomegranate juice," said the parrot.

Night was falling. So Eugene curled up under a
palm tree and fell asleep.

When he woke up, the parrot was drawing
a diagram in the sand.

"What's that?"

"Our boat," said the parrot.

"Terrific," said Eugene. "And who's going to build it?"

"You are," said the parrot.

VANE

MASTHEAD
FITTING

HALYARD

HEAD GAFF

CONSTRUCTION
PLAN

12'

MAST

90°

TACK BOOM TILLER CLEW

MAST
COAT

5'3"

12'6½"

BENCH RUDDER

KEEL
SLOT

3'6"

2'5¾"

CENTERBOARD
TRUNK

This parrot seemed to know a lot about boats, so
Eugene decided to give it a shot.
First, the parrot told him how to put the hull together.
Next, the parrot told him how to rig the rudder.

Then the parrot told him how to connect the centerboard and secure the mast.

"Terrific," said Eugene. "I'm going to permanently damage my lower back."

But in no time at all, he finished the boat!
"Good job," said the parrot. "Now all we need is the sail."
"Terrific," said Eugene. "And where do you expect to find a sail?"
"You're wearing it," said the parrot.

"Terrific," said Eugene. "This coat cost me thirty-two dollars."

When the tide was right, Eugene grabbed a few pomegranates and the two castaways shoved off.

But soon the wind died down. For hours and hours,
Eugene and the parrot drifted under the hot sun.
All their pomegranates were gone.
"Terrific," said Eugene. "We're going to die of thirst."

"Wait a second," said the parrot. "There's a ship."
"Ship?" said Eugene. "What ship?"
"*Look out!*" said the parrot.

KA-BANG! An old fishing trawler smashed into their boat, and Eugene and the parrot went splashing into the sea.

Luckily, one of the fishermen spotted them and hauled them in.

"Look, fellas," said the captain. "It's Lenny."
"Uh, I'm not Lenny," said Eugene.
"Not you!" said the captain. "The parrot! We lost
  that dumb bird in a storm the other day."

"Listen here," said Eugene. "Your parrot isn't dumb.
  He saved my life! He told me how to build our boat!"
"You're nuts," said the captain. "Lenny doesn't talk.
  He can't even say 'Polly wants a cracker'!"

"Of course he talks," said Eugene. "Isn't that right, Lenny? . . . Lenny? . . . Lenny?"
The captain grabbed the parrot. "Mister," he said, "you've been out in the sun too long."

It was true, Eugene was totally exhausted. So he found a place to lie down and immediately fell asleep.

When Eugene woke up the next morning, he couldn't believe his eyes. The boat was docked in Bermuda!

"Okay, pal," said the captain. "This is where you get off. We're heading out."

"Where's Lenny?" said Eugene.

"Beats me. That darn bird is gone again."

When the boat pulled away, Eugene was the only one left on the pier.

Except for a parrot.
"Lenny!" said Eugene. "Your boat's leaving! What are you waiting for?"
"You."

Lenny hopped onto Eugene's shoulder. And what do you think Eugene said?